RIVER THAMES

HIGH ST.

Greenwich
Pier

ROYAL
NAVAL COLLEGE

TRAFALGAR RD.

NATIONAL
MARITIME
MUSEUM

Greenwich
Station

Greenwich
Park

GREENWICH RD

Ashburnham Pl.

OLD ROYAL
OBSERVATORY

Time for Horatio

Written by Penelope Colville Paine

Illustrated by Itoko Maeno

Advocacy Press, Santa Barbara

For my family

*Special thanks to Mindy Bingham, Sandy Stryker,
William Sheehan, Linda Wagner, Stephanie Galindo, Michael Rose,
Josie Godden, Helen Exley, Maud Bartlett, Jayne Caldwell, Anna Tolchard,
Brian Davis and Donna Massello-Chiacos.*

Text Copyright © 1990 by Penelope Colville Paine
Illustration Copyright © 1990 by Itoko Maeno

 Published by Advocacy Press
P.O. Box 236
Santa Barbara, California 93102 USA

*Advocacy Press is a division of the Girls Club of Greater Santa Barbara, an affiliate of
Girls Clubs of America, Inc.*

Book layout by Christine Nolt

Library of Congress Cataloging-in-Publication Data

Paine, Penelope Colville, 1946-
  Time for Horatio.
  Summary: Puzzled by a world of confrontation, competition, and aggression,
Horatio the cat seeks a way to cultivate harmony.

    [1. Cats—Fiction. 2. Conduct of life—Fiction. 3. London (England)—Fiction].
I. Maeno, Itoko, ill. II. Title.
PZ7.P163Ti 1990   [Fic]   89-18304
ISBN 0-911655-33-6

Printed in Hong Kong

His heart still pounded after the narrow escape. The dog had finally gone away. As the kitten peered into the morning fog, opening his eyes slowly to see where he was hiding, he found himself looking at a row of very large teeth. Certain that he was about to be eaten by yet another ferocious beast, he squealed in terror, leaped high in the air and landed in front of two rapidly approaching bicycles.

"What on earth!" shouted Charlie, skidding to a halt.

"Dad, it's a kitten, " gasped Oliver, inspecting the quivering mass of wet fur. "Can we take it home with us?"

"Now, what would you want with a scrap-of-a-thing like that?" his father asked gruffly. "It's no good to anyone. Come on. I've got work to do."

"Dad, don't be so mean. I've always wanted a kitten. This one is lost and alone and needs someone to love him." Oliver gently tucked the little animal into his pocket before his father could say no.

6

As they passed the statue of Admiral Lord Nelson, one of England's most famous naval heroes, Oliver called up to the stone figure, "What do you think, Lord Nelson, shall I name my kitten after you?"

"Well," scoffed Charlie, "Lord Nelson was a pretty important person. I doubt that this kitten can live up to the name."

"I know he's special," said Oliver. As they rode off towards Whitehall, he sang a song to Horatio that he had learned at Nelson School.

Horatio was a weakling
When a very little boy was he.
They never thought he'd rise to be
An important man on the mighty sea.
But there he stands
In Trafalgar Square,
High up aloft
So that all may stare.
And here and now we all declare
He's the TALLEST man in England.

"Here we are, Horatio," whispered Oliver. He coaxed the sleepy kitten out of his pocket. "Welcome to Charlie Bibbs' Pleasure Steamers. We make daily river trips to Greenwich aboard our boat, the *Victorious*."

Oliver laid Horatio in a box cushioned with his school scarf. Safe at last, Horatio started to close his eyes. Suddenly a loud noise from above jolted them open. BONG! . . .BONG! . . . BONG! . . .BONG! . . . BONG!

Horatio leaped up! Oliver gathered the startled kitten and held him close. "Easy, Horatio, that's just Big Ben," he said softly, stroking the kitten. "It's probably the most famous clock in the world. People in many countries hear it strike the hour on their radios. Do you know that just a few coins on the pendulum keep Big Ben balanced and precisely on time?"

Oliver's words were of little comfort. It was all too much for Horatio — being chased by that horrid dog, then the lion's teeth, Charlie's gruffness and now a loud clock. Exhausted, he fell into a deep sleep. Even Big Ben's chimes couldn't wake him.

Oliver took good care of Horatio and, in a couple of days, he was much stronger. One bright morning Horatio woke to discover a long line of tourists waiting to board the *Victorious*. Charlie brought the engines to life. *Chug-a-chug-a, chug-a-chug-a,* they spluttered. Oliver untied the heavy ropes. "Come on, Horatio," he called, "it's the first day of the tourist season, and I'm going to show you Greenwich."

The *Victorious* pushed out into the middle of the Thames. Hoping to view his new surroundings, Horatio tried to walk along the deck. But the deck was rolling with the motion of the water. In fact, everything was moving. Horatio's feet kept slipping and sliding. He felt dizzy and his tummy ached. He wondered how the river, which had always looked so smooth, could do this to him. The *Victorious* lurched again, sending Horatio skidding along the deck.

10

Charlie chuckled to himself and called over to Oliver.

"Look," as he pointed to Horatio, "I do believe your admiral is seasick!"

"Oh dear, Horatio" Oliver sighed, "You do look rather ill."

Oliver turned to the passengers. "Please don't laugh at my kitten! Can't you see he feels awful? This is Horatio's first voyage, and he has to get used to the motion."

"Why don't you come forward with me, Horatio, away from all this mean teasing," Oliver coaxed. Carefully, he helped Horatio wobble along the swaying deck.

That was only the first of many upsets for Horatio. A wasp didn't want to share spilled ice cream so it stung Horatio's nose.

The ravens that live at the Tower of London squawked loudly to warn Horatio that they'd bite if he wasn't careful when he visited the Tower.

When he didn't want to sit on her lap, a little girl pulled his tail.

As Horatio peeked out from under a bench, a boy squirted him with a water pistol. There seemed to be no end to Horatio's problems.

Hoping to make a friend, Horatio meowed excitedly to a passing seagull as the boat approached Tower Bridge. The seagull replied with a menacing squawk and swooped down over Horatio's head. Horatio was so startled he nearly fell overboard.

"Horatio, what a scaredy-cat you are!" Charlie scoffed, "Look at you with a swollen nose and watery eyes! You need to stand up for yourself like I do. No one pushes me around! They'd be sorry if they did." Charlie waved his fist firmly, grimacing as the kitten backed away.

"Don't mind him," said Oliver. "You know Dad. He thinks everyone should be tough and gruff."

Just then the engines slowed to a stop as the *Victorious* docked at Greenwich. "All ashore for Greenwich!" called Charlie. After lowering the gangway and helping the passengers off, Oliver put Horatio on his shoulder and set out to explore the town.

At the Maritime Museum, Horatio looked into the glass cases as he and Oliver walked through the exhibit rooms. They were full of old guns, cannons and stuffed models. Old paintings lined the walls.

In one corner Horatio recognized a painting of Admiral Nelson. My namesake, he thought, as he strained for a better look.

A tourist, distracted by the kitten, bumped into Oliver and the two lurched forward. "Oops!" he apologized. Just inches away, Nelson's steely eye stared right at Horatio! Sure that he was in imminent danger again, Horatio jumped down from his perch and dashed off frantically seeking a safe place to hide.

"Horatio, where are you?" Oliver called out softly, worried that the guard might see his kitten. Behind him, he heard very strange sounds coming from an old cannon. Turning around, he saw Horatio disappear into its dusty barrel. The dust made Horatio sneeze so hard he tumbled backwards to the floor.

"Poor Horatio," Oliver said, picking up the kitten and brushing him off. "Perhaps you'll like the Observatory and the park. I don't think anything mean can happen to you there."

The Royal Observatory was filled with displays of all sorts of clocks and timepieces. In one strange room, a giant telescope poked out of the roof and a big map of the world covered one wall.

"Look, Horatio," explained Oliver, "this is where we are . . . here on this middle line." He pointed to a spot on the red line marked with a zero. "Scientists have divided the world up into strips . . . a bit like an orange."

Oliver, who always had things in his pocket, pulled out a battered orange and proceeded to peel it and remove a segment. "Because the starting point is here in Greenwich, they call this line the Greenwich meridian." But to Horatio, the world looked awfully big stretched out on the wall and not a bit like the round orange.

"Here's the line," Oliver said as he carried Horatio outside. The courtyard was crossed by a long, shiny strip.

"It divides the eastern half of the world from the western half. Look! I can put one foot on each side."

Oliver hopped from one side to the other. "People all over the world set their time by the official clock here. Even Big Ben is set by this clock. When it's lunch time here, it's breakfast time in New York and tea time in Moscow. It's called Greenwich MEAN Time."

Horatio looked up with startled eyes and backed away, meowing loudly and swishing his tail back and forth. The unhappy kitten didn't quite understand all this about east and west but he did understand MEAN.

At first Oliver was puzzled by Horatio's actions, but then he smiled understandingly. "Oh, Horatio, I said MEAN, didn't I! Like the wasp and the boy with the squirt gun. Perhaps it's because the world is running on MEAN time that everyone gets so upset, fights and doesn't want to share."

"And speaking of time," Oliver continued as he glanced at his watch, "it's time for us to get going or we'll miss the boat."

22

Back on board the *Victorious,* the two adventurers were lulled into their own thoughts by the warm sunshine and water lapping the side of the boat.

Suddenly, Horatio started to twist and stretch.

"Horatio, stop wiggling!" Oliver said as the kitten struggled out of his arms. "What has come over you?"

Oliver looked down at his kitten. Something strange about the look in Horatio's eye startled Oliver. Horatio was obviously agitated. He paced back and forth meowing loudly. As soon as Charlie docked the boat, Horatio leaped onto the quay and ran up the street.

"Horatio! Wait for me!" cried Oliver, as he scrambled off the boat and tried to catch up with his kitten.

Horatio didn't even look back. He ran like a cat with a purpose, darting around cars and people. Nothing would stop him.

Before long, Horatio reached the base of Big Ben's tower. The door was slightly ajar. Slipping through, he started to climb the steps, one and then two at a time, all the way to the top.

On a platform in the belfry, Horatio stopped to catch his breath. Looking up, he saw that the giant hammer was ready to strike the hour. The quarter bells started to chime.

Horatio flattened his ears from the deafening sound. His whole body vibrated so much he had to wind his tail around the railing to keep from falling.

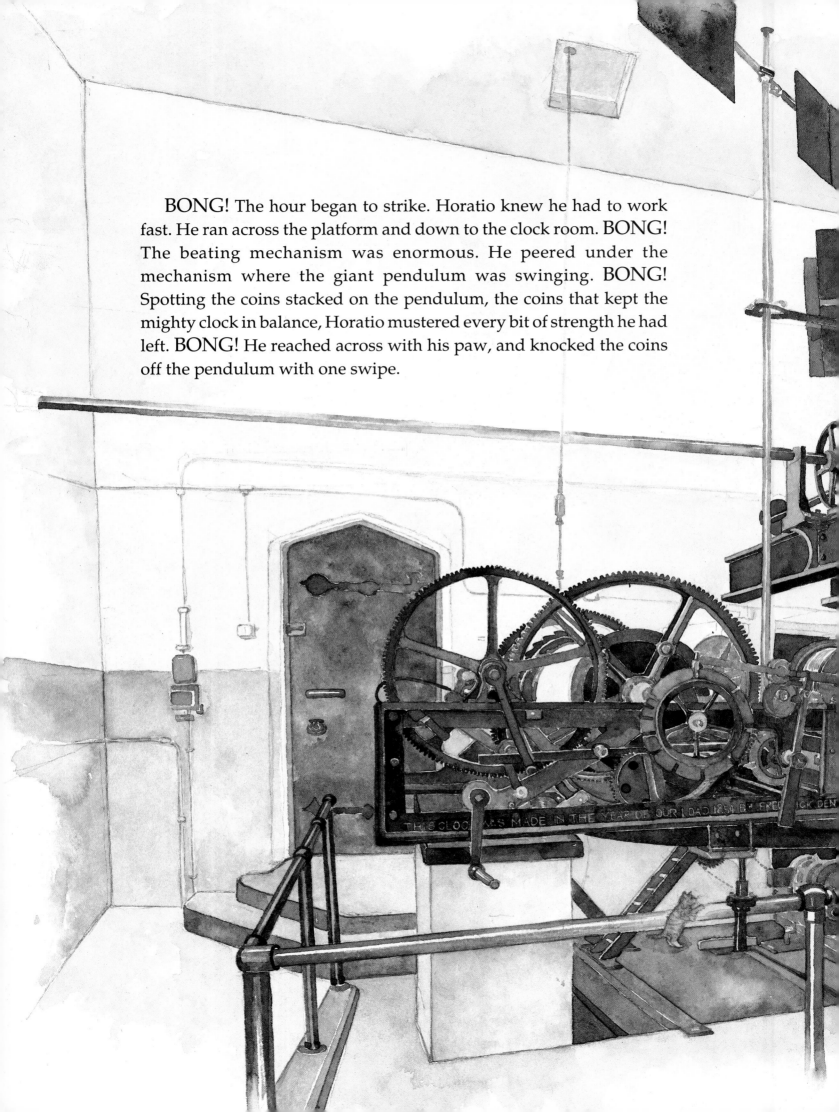

BONG! The hour began to strike. Horatio knew he had to work fast. He ran across the platform and down to the clock room. BONG! The beating mechanism was enormous. He peered under the mechanism where the giant pendulum was swinging. BONG! Spotting the coins stacked on the pendulum, the coins that kept the mighty clock in balance, Horatio mustered every bit of strength he had left. BONG! He reached across with his paw, and knocked the coins off the pendulum with one swipe.

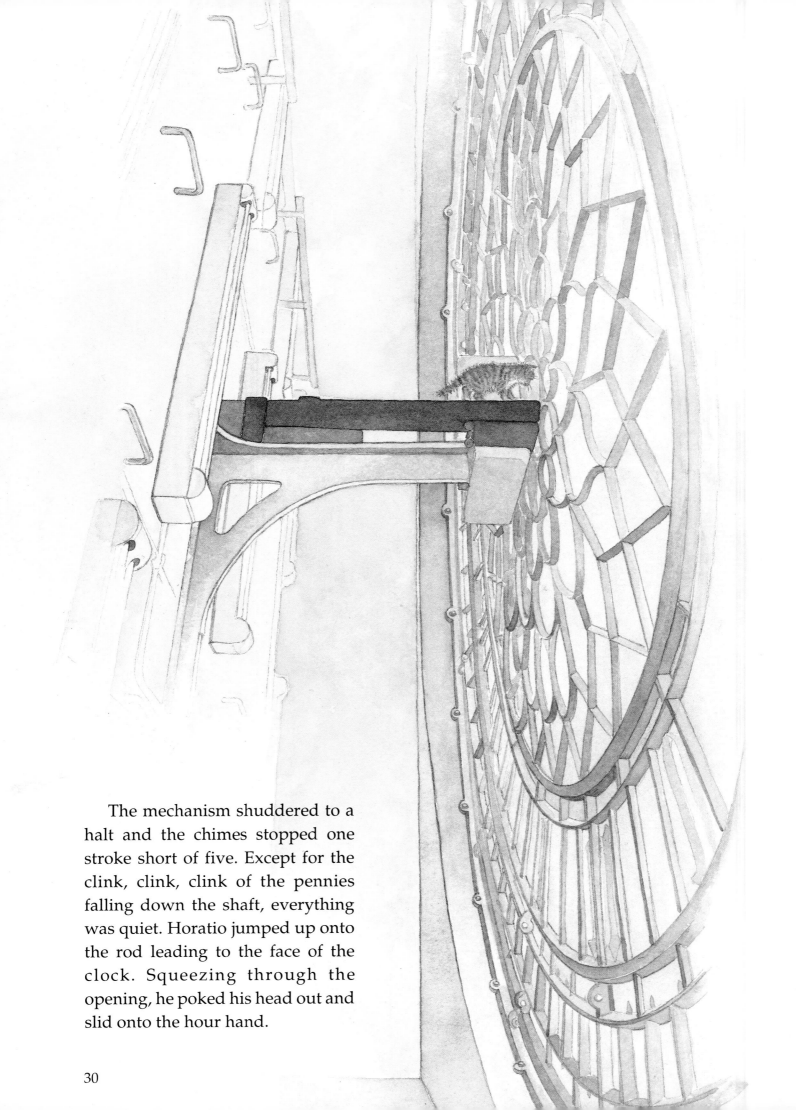

The mechanism shuddered to a halt and the chimes stopped one stroke short of five. Except for the clink, clink, clink of the pennies falling down the shaft, everything was quiet. Horatio jumped up onto the rod leading to the face of the clock. Squeezing through the opening, he poked his head out and slid onto the hour hand.

Horatio peered down from his perch 180 feet above the street. He could see Oliver in the middle of what was already becoming quite a crowd of people.

"What happened?" asked a passerby. "There were only four strokes but it's five o'clock!"

"Look!" screamed someone else, "There is a kitten hanging on the hour hand!"

Oliver, who had been searching for his kitten, looked up in amazement.

"It's my kitten!" he shouted, squinting to see better. "Yes, yes, it's Horatio!"

"He's stopped the clock," said a policeman who had joined the group. "Why would he do that?"

"I don't . . ." but Oliver stopped short. As he remembered his words to Horatio while they were in Greenwich, it suddenly all made sense. "Horatio stopped the clock because he's trying to stop time . . . MEAN time!" Oliver gasped.

"Pardon me," interrupted another person, "but WHAT does that have to do with Big Ben?"

"Well," continued Oliver, "Horatio has mixed up mean *actions* with mean *time*. He's really a friendly kitten but all sorts of unkind things have happened to him. He knows Big Ben tells the time for people all over the world!"

"What an incredible cat," exclaimed a woman in a sari. "If we all cared that much, things could change."

Oliver cupped his hands and called up to Horatio. "Hang on tightly, Horatio. We'll get you down."

There was a great deal of commotion. Fire engines arrived, and long ladders were raised up to the big clock face. Carefully, a firefighter climbed up and retrieved Horatio.

"And here is Horatio!" A television reporter said as she turned to the rescued kitten. "At exactly 5 p.m. today he stopped, . . . umm . . . augh . . . MEAN time." Horatio snuggled into Oliver's arms as the reporter continued. "Found in Trafalgar Square just six days ago, Horatio's experiences — which have been far from pleasant — have led him to believe that the world should run on . . .", she smiled, "KIND time."

Someone from the crowd shouted, "Three cheers for Horatio!"

"Is that your son's kitten?" the policeman asked Charlie, who was just joining the crowd. "You must be proud of him. He certainly stood up for himself today . . . and for everyone else, too."

"Well . . . er . . . yes," answered Charlie, "That's right. You could say he did that."

The news flashed around the world about the kitten that wanted to stop
MEAN time. People everywhere started to think . . .

. . . of ways that they could be kinder.

BONG! BONG! Oliver woke up with a start. He rubbed his eyes and looked up at the big clock face and then down at Horatio, asleep on his lap. They were still aboard the *Victorious*. Charlie and a group of tourists were standing over him. "Dad," he shouted, "Big Ben . . . the time . . . he's striking . . . Horatio, you're here . . . where are the reporters?"

"What reporters? What are you talking about? A lot of help you are!" Charlie grumbled as he pulled Oliver to his feet. "I've been looking everywhere for you and here you are day dreaming."

"A dream! Yes, that's what it was, Dad. But a wonderful dream." Oliver's eyes beamed as he told the story to the group of people on the boat.

"Just think of what it would be like if we really could stop all the MEANNESS!" Oliver mused as he finished his tale. "All sorts of things could happen . . . ."

"Instead of fighting people could be dancing . . . ."

"Instead of shouting people could sing," a little girl chimed in.

"Ha, ha, burglars could give back the things that they stole," a man in a green sweater added, chuckling at the thought. Soon everyone was calling out ideas.

"Guns could fire party favors," said someone.

"Missiles could turn into doves," said another.

"Mrs. Smith's dog could lick the mailcarrier instead of biting him," said Charlie.

"Yes, yes Dad!" said Oliver, "And just think, you could even take a liking to Horatio!" Charlie started to protest but . . .

. . . he was enjoying the attention, and everyone seemed to agree. "I don't know about you, or your precious cat," he said to Oliver as he picked up Horatio, "but I can't say that I have ever thought of KIND time. Perhaps it's time . . . time for Horatio!"

Oliver smiled up at his father. "Dad, I know the first thing we can do to help make a kinder world."

The next day the *Victorious* received a new name.

Admiral Lord Nelson
Pages 7, 18
Regarded as one of the world's greatest admirals, Lord Horatio Nelson was born in Norfolk in 1758. Although a sickly child, at age 12 he requested a place on the gunship *Raisonnable* commanded by his uncle. He learned his trade well and soon gained rank in the British Royal Navy. Nelson was fatally wounded aboard *H.M.S. Victory* during the Battle of Trafalgar in 1805.

Trafalgar Square
Pages 5, 7
Named about 1835, Trafalgar Square was laid out on the site of the Kings Mews. The Nelson Column which dominates the square is one of London's most famous landmarks.

Nelson's Song
Page 7
An original song probably written in the 1940s for Nelson Primary School, Twickenham, Middlesex.

The Great Westminster Clock
Pages 4, 8, 25, 26, 27, 28-29, 30, 31, 32, 34, 42
Housed in the Clock Tower of the Houses of Parliament, the Great Westminster Clock was constructed and installed in 1858. It is the largest and most accurate public clock in the world. To maintain absolute accuracy, the clock's time is automatically telegraphed, twice daily, to the Greenwich Observatory (now located in Herstmonceux Castle, Sussex). The pendulum is regulated by the addition or subtraction of very small weights, usually old English pennies and crowns. Each of the four clock faces is 23 feet in diameter and 180 feet from the ground.

Big Ben
Page 27
The nickname given to the giant bell on which the great Westminster Clock strikes. First heard in 1859, Big Ben weighs 13-1/2 tons. One theory reports that the bell was named after then Commissioner of Works, Sir Benjamin Hall. There are 334 steps leading up to the belfry. Four quarter bells sound a chime arranged from George Frederic Handel's *Messiah*. Every hour the first blow on Big Ben denotes the correct time. The bell was first heard worldwide on the radio in 1923 and first viewed on television New Year's Eve 1949.

Tower of London
(Backcover)
Built by William the Conqueror from 1086-1097 to protect and control the City of London, additions have been made throughout the centuries. It has been used as a fortress, a palace and a prison. Housing the Crown Jewels, the Tower of London is a vital part of British history.

The Ravens
Page 12
Ravens were once common in London streets, and they were protected for the services they rendered as scavengers. There have probably always been ravens at the Tower of London, and there is a legend that the Tower will fall should they ever leave. For this reason the birds are carefully guarded and cared for by the Yeoman Quartermaster. There are six permanent resident ravens, and each receives a weekly allowance of food. Often very noisy and known to damage parked cars, the ravens do not hesitate to take the odd peck at unsuspecting visitors!

Tower Bridge
Pages 14-15
The first and only bridge down river from London Bridge, Tower Bridge was opened in 1894. It is a bascule bridge opening to allow shipping to pass underneath. A high level footbridge allowed pedestrians to cross while the main span is raised.

Greenwich Maritime Museum
Pages 18, 19
Located in the Queens House designed by Inigo Jones, and in the old Royal Hospital School buildings, the Museum first opened in 1937. It is considered the largest and finest of its kind in the world.

The Royal Greenwich Observatory
Built in 1675 during the reign of Charles II, the building was designed by Sir Christopher Wren. A royal warrant appointed John Flamsteed as the 'astronomical observator' to research possible ways to measure time and distance accurately.

Longitude and Latitude
Page 20
Zero degrees longitude, the prime meridian, runs north and south through Greenwich. Zero degrees latitude runs east-west and is marked by the Equator. Latitude lines circle the globe parallel to the Equator between the North and South Poles. Longitude lines run from the North Pole to the South Pole around the globe.

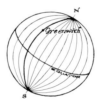

Greenwich Meridian / Prime Meridian   Pages 20, 21
At the International Conference held in Washington, D.C. in 1884, it was agreed that the meridian (line of longitude) passing through the Royal Observatory, at Greenwich, England, should be the zero or prime meridian. This meridian is used universally for timekeeping and navigation on land, at sea and in the air.

Greenwich Time Ball
Page 22
Installed in 1833 on the roof of Flamsteed House adjacent to the Royal Observatory, the Greenwich Time Ball was the first visual time signal. The ball still drops at precisely 1:00 p.m. (GMT) every day.

Greenwich Mean Time (GMT)
The correct time at Greenwich, England is the basis of the International Time Zone System. For example, when it is 12:00 noon in London (0° degrees), it is only 7:00 a.m. in New York (73° 50' west). Time zones adjust in complete hours.

Mean: noun;
average, middle position

Mean: adjective;
disagreeable, selfish, offensive, bad tempered and unaccommodating

Children today live in a violent and frightening world. In spite of the horrors of history we still glorify aggression. By the time an American child is 16, he or she has witnessed 200,000 acts of violence on television. Toys, games and the media encourage boys, especially, to get what they want through physical and verbal force rather than through intelligence, persuasion, tact, compassion or skill.

Society imposes "macho" roles on even the youngest boys. Parents, too, perhaps unconsciously, often discourage their sons from showing emotion or crying. Children learn not to show weakness for fear of being scorned as sissies by their peers. Once ingrained, these lessons are difficult to purge when the boy becomes the man, the child the father. And the world keeps turning.

President George Bush acknowledged the contaminating atmosphere of narrow-minded hostility in calling for a kinder, gentler nation. *Time for Horatio* calls for a kinder, gentler world. Horatio is a hero for our time because a kinder, gentler world does not need people who are weak and ineffective. Quite the contrary. It requires a population of Horatios able to turn away from violence, willing to stand up for the weak, ready to work for a world where peace can be taken for granted and all living things are treated with respect.

As Sey Chassler, consulting editor of *Parade Magazine*, says, "We must stop thinking about life as some contest to be won, rather as important work to be done together."

People everywhere long for the opportunity and leadership that will enable them to lead peaceful lives. *Time for Horatio* is a starting point for parents who want their children to take up the challenge.

You might ask these questions:

How did Horatio get people to think about a kinder world?

What is the new name of Charlie's boat?

Why did Oliver and Charlie change the name of the boat?

Can you think of something kind you can do?

Encourage children to:

- become aware of their feelings and express them constructively.
- discuss history in terms other than violent events and wars.
- participate in the arts, non-competitive sports, and environmental projects.
- see the negative aspects of bullying and territorial concerns.
- value sharing and cooperation over conquering.

And:

Through projects and discussions encourage children to actively promote a peaceful and more responsible world.

Help children accept and respect differences through exposure to different cultures and religions.

Show children how to lose with dignity and win with grace.

Emphasize that people of all ages and cultures are important and that their ideas have value.

Penelope Colville Paine

From Twickenham, England, Penelope Colville Paine attended Goldsmiths' College, University of London, where she received a B.A. in Fine Arts. In 1987 she co-authored with Mindy Bingham *My Way Sally*, the winner of the 1989 Ben Franklin Award. Keenly interested in issues facing girls and women, Penelope became aware of the need for similar messages of equity for boys. She and her husband John have five children—Dan, John, Diane, Oliver and Miles.

Itoko Maeno

Itoko Maeno is the illustrator of the best-seller *Minou* and award-winning *My Way Sally* and *Tonia the Tree*. Born in Tokyo, Japan, she received her Bachelor's degree in Graphic Design from Tama Art University. While researching *Time for Horatio*, Itoko was treated to a special tour of The Great Westminster Clock (Big Ben). Itoko's attention to detail and artistic view point will charm as well as educate.

Books by Advocacy Press

Minou, written by Mindy Bingham, illustrated by Itoko Maeno. Hardcover with dust jacket, 64 pages with full-color illustrations throughout. ISBN 0-911655-36-0. $14.95.

My Way Sally, by Mindy Bingham and Penelope Paine, illustrated by Itoko Maeno. Hardcover with dust jacket, 48 pages with full-color illustrations throughout. ISBN 0-911655-27-1. $13.95.

Father Gander Nursery Rhymes: The Equal Rhymes Amendment, by Father Gander. Hardcover with dust jacket, full-color illustrations throughout, 48 pages. ISBN 0-911655-12-3. $14.95.

Tonia the Tree, by Sandy Stryker, illustrations by Itoko Maeno. Hardcover with dust jacket, 32 pages with full-color illustrations throughout. ISBN 0-911655-16-6. $13.95.

Kylie's Song, by Patty Sheehan, illustrated by Itoko Maeno. Hardcover with dust jacket, 32 pages with full-color illustrations throughout. ISBN 0-911655-19-0. $13.95.

Berta Benz and the Motorwagen, written by Mindy Bingham, illustrated by Itoko Maeno. Hardcover with dust jacket, 48 pages with full-color illustrations throughout. ISBN 0-911655-38-7. $14.95.

Time for Horatio, written by Penelope Paine, illustrated by Itoko Maeno. Hardcover with dust jacket, 48 pages with full-color illustrations throughout. ISBN 0-911655-33-6. $14.95.

Choices: A Teen Woman's Journal for Self-awareness and Personal Planning, by Mindy Bingham, Judy Edmondson and Sandy Stryker. Softcover, 240 pages. ISBN 0-911655-22-0. $14.95.

Challenges: A Young Man's Journal for Self-awareness and Personal Planning, by Bingham, Edmondson and Stryker. Softcover, 240 pages. ISBN 0-911655-24-7. $14.95.

More Choices: A Strategic Planning Guide for Mixing Career and Family, by Mindy Bingham and Sandy Stryker. Softcover, 240 pages. ISBN 0-911655-28-X. $15.95.

Changes: A Woman's Journal for Self-awareness and Personal Planning, by Mindy Bingham, Sandy Stryker and Judy Edmondson. Softcover, 240 pages. ISBN 0-911655-40-9. $14.95.

Mother-Daughter Choices: A Handbook for the Coordinator, by Mindy Bingham, Lari Quinn and William Sheehan. Softcover, 144 pages. ISBN 0-911655-44-1. $7.95.

Women Helping Girls with Choices, by Mindy Bingham and Sandy Stryker. Softcover, 192 pages. ISBN 0-911655-00-X. $9.95.

You can find these books at better bookstores. Or you may order them directly by sending a check for the amount shown above (California residents add 6.25% sales tax), plus $3.00 each for shipping and handling, to Advocacy Press, P.O. Box 236, Dept. H, Santa Barbara, California 93102. For your review, we will be happy to send you more information on these publications. Proceeds from the sale of these books will benefit and contribute to the further development of programs for girls and young women.